The Adventures of Quinton the Quarter

Written by **John Maulhardt**

Illustrated by **Peaches Olson**

A Child's First Book About Money

THE ADVENTURES OF QUINTON THE QUARTER

Copyright ©1995 by Simple Wisdom Press

The character Quinton the Quarter™ is a trademark of Simple Wisdom Press.

Published by Simple Wisdom Press
791 Price St., Suite 273
Pismo Beach, CA 93449

ISBN 0-9637822-9-0
Library of Congress Catalog Card Number: 93-86641

Printed in Hong Kong

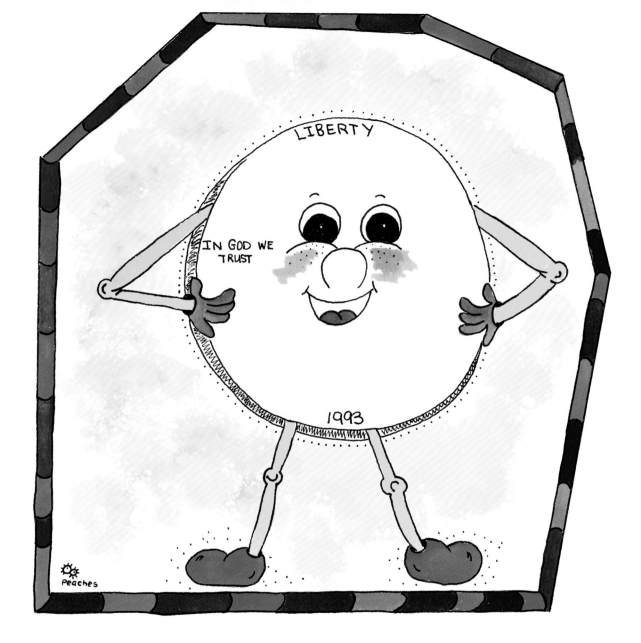

Everyone in the world would know when and where Quinton the Quarter was born because his birth date and place were clearly stamped right on his shiny little face.

How proud Quinton felt as he came out of the coin press and was packed together in a tight roll with thirty-nine other shiny new quarters. As he was being loaded into a money bag for shipping, Quinton wondered just what this new world would be like that he was about to enter.

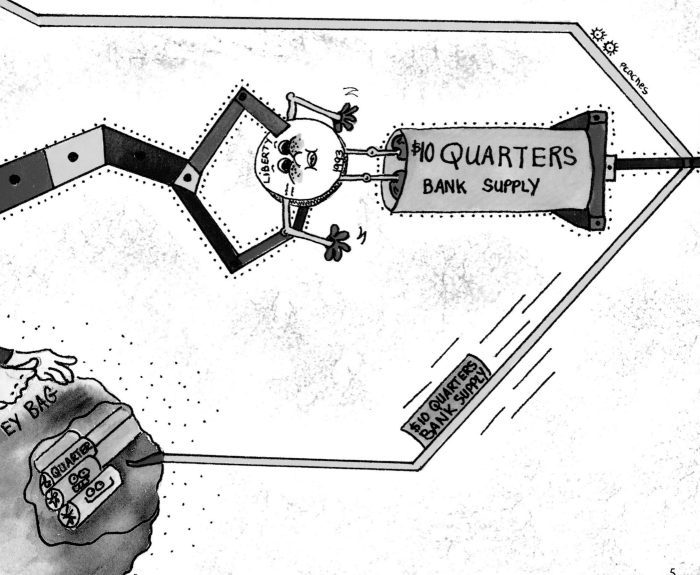

Quinton knew that he was something special and that he was something people would prize and value, for he was worth much more than the mixture of copper and nickel metals that made him up. With Quinton, anyone could buy twenty-five cents worth of anything.

Before Quinton could be spent he had to do some traveling.

Quinton and his friends were loaded into a very heavy steel truck. The truck was protected by armed guards because he and his other money friends were so valuable.

How important Quinton felt as he headed for his first stop, the big Federal Reserve Bank building. Here money like Quinton was stored before being passed on to the local community banks, like the one perhaps your family uses.

The next day, Quinton was taken to a neighborhood bank where the people of the town stored their money when they were not using it.

Quinton was placed in a drawer with all sorts of other money. Around him were other coins of different sizes and values, and behind him were neat stacks of paper money, each one worth many Quintons.

Together they all waited, but for what? He wondered?

Quinton was about to find out, as a customer came into the bank and wrote out a special piece of paper called a "check" to withdraw some of his money.

In exchange for his check, Quinton and some of his pals were carefully counted out by the bank teller. The man was a store owner who was going to use Quinton to make change when people used paper money at his grocery store.

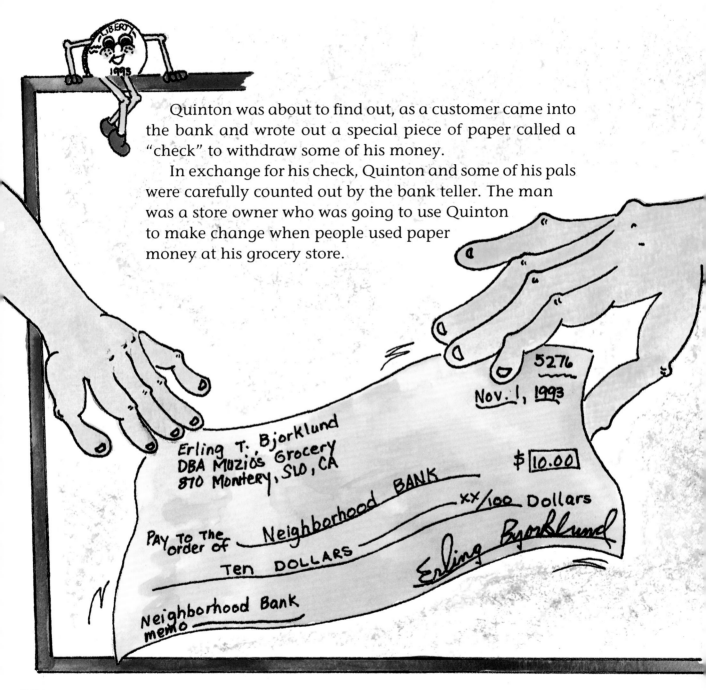

5276

Nov. 1, 1993

Erling T. Bjorklund
DBA Muzios Grocery
870 Monterey, SLO, CA

$ 10.00

PAY TO THE order of _____ Neighborhood BANK _____ xx/100 Dollars

Ten DOLLARS

Erling Bjorklund

Neighborhood Bank
memo _____

What a busy place the store was. Customers were coming and going all day long. Quinton sat in the money drawer with the other coins and bills anxiously waiting for it to be his turn to be passed on.

Finally a woman selected a magazine that cost seventy-five cents. To pay for the magazine, she gave the store clerk a one dollar bill. As the woman was owed twenty-five cents in return, Quinton was taken from the drawer and given to the woman as change.

Slipping Quinton into her purse, the woman left the store and hurried down the street.

But then she did a very careless thing.

As the woman was in a big hurry to pick up some packages, she threw Quinton and her purse into the back seat of her car, leaving him out for anyone to see.

Quinton was suddenly startled by the crashing
of glass as a big dirty glove reached in through the
car window and grabbed the purse . . . and Quinton too!
A shocked Quinton realized that he was being stolen!

Next thing he knew, a very scared Quinton was thrown into a bag and was charging down the street.

Oh, why would some people do such awful things just to try and get their hands on him, he thought.

After a long trip, Quinton was finally pulled from the bag. But to his surprise, instead of being used to buy a sandwich or a soda, he was shoved into a narrow slot on a big noisy machine with lots of flashing lights and a spinning dial.
This was not a grocery store!

The man pulled a big handle on the side of the machine and Quinton went tumbling down onto a huge pile of many other quarters.

One of the quarters told a puzzled Quinton that many people put quarters into the machine day and night, trying to get it to let go of all its money. But the machine was set to keep most of the quarters it was given, and only now and then did it ever give a few of them back.

What a silly way for people to spend their time, Quinton thought. Especially when he learned that even when they were tired and hungry, many people would not stop gambling with their money, trying to get lots of quarters for very little work.

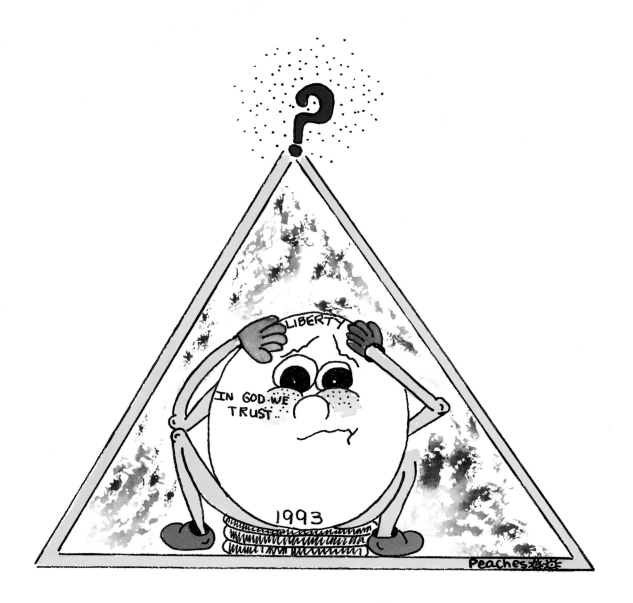

Quinton realized now that there were many greedy people in the world who would cheat, steal, lie, and do almost anything for money.

Oh, there just HAD to be a better way for him to be used.

And as Quinton got older, he did find out that people could spend him in many useful ways . . .

And that there was much for him to do.

One day, after many more journeys and many more owners, Quinton found himself being given to a little boy by his dad for helping him.

peaches

The boy's family had taught him to save his money, and so Quinton was put into the boy's piggy bank with lots of other coins. Quinton had never been saved before.

The other coins told him that the boy regularly emptied his piggy bank and took the coins to the big bank downtown for safe keeping.

An excited Quinton knew all about the bank, for it was his first home.

Peaches O.

At the bank, the boy's money was put together with lots of other people's money. Then when other people needed to buy something, like a boat or a house or a car, they could borrow this money from the bank, if they promised to pay it back.

The bank also promised to pay the boy back his money, plus a little bit extra for letting them use it. This little bit extra was called "interest."

In this way, the boy's money would grow a little bit each day, and someday HE would have enough money to buy his own bike, or perhaps a car, or maybe even enough money to help pay his way through college.

The boy's father was very proud of him for the way he saved and took care of his money.

One day, Quinton and all the other coins were taken out of the piggy bank and put in the boy's best pants pocket.

Quinton expected to be taken to the bank, but he was in for a surprise.

Instead of going to the bank, Quinton went with the boy and his whole family to their local community church for Sunday services.

The church was having a fund drive to collect money to help the poor and hungry of their town, and soon Quinton was eagerly being put into the collection basket by the generous boy.

This made the boy's family even more proud of him.

And it soon made Quinton feel very proud also, for in no time at all, he was being used to buy groceries for the town's poor and hungry people.

Now Quinton felt even more special and really good about himself, because he found out that people could also use him in many caring and generous ways if they wanted to.

31

Quinton could be used by people not only to be spent on themselves, but also to help other people live better lives too!